Taking care of the environment is a responsibility every Georgia citizen must embrace and an important character lesson we have to teach our children.

I remember my daddy telling me that we had better take care of the world we live in – it is the only one we are getting. At the time, I did not fully understand what he was saying. Now I understand completely how important it is to teach young children, in terms they can understand, about the environment.

This book will provide children and parents with many wonderful learning opportunities. What a marvelous way to educate Pre-K children about endangered animals, provide them with ideas on how they can participate in saving the environment and help them practice their pre-math skills!

I hope you read this book and many others to your children often. You are your child's first teacher, and the time you spend together will be invaluable to both of you. Reading together can be one of the first of many shared memories. I know it has been for my wife, my children and me.

Roy E. Barnes

Roy E. Barnes
Governor

3 Pandas Planting

by Megan Halsey

Simon & Schuster Books for Young Readers

SIMON & SCHUSTER BOOKS FOR YOUNG READERS
An imprint of Simon & Schuster Children's Publishing Division
1230 Avenue of the Americas
New York, NY 10020

The text for this book is set in ITC Caslon No. 224 Book.
The illustrations are rendered in gouache and gesso, with pen-and-ink line work,
and colored pencil and pastels used for shading and detail.

Printed and bound in the United States of America

Library of Congress Cataloging-in-Publication Data
Halsey, Megan.
3 pandas planting : counting down to help the earth / by Megan Halsey.
p.   cm.
ISBN 0-02-742035-3
1. Counting—Juvenile literature.   2. Animals—Juvenile literature.
3. Ecology—Juvenile literature.
[1. Counting. 2. Environmental protection.] I. Title.
QA113.H36   1994
513.2'11—dc20   93-22971
ISBN 0-689-83305-9 (SSBFYR edition)

This book is dedicated to
all the friends of the earth.

12 Crocodiles

We're carpooling.

A
B
2
A+

11 Tigers

We turn off
our faucets.

10 Otters

We're organized:
bottles in one bin,
trash in another.

9 Turtles

We take our
cans home.

8 Condors

We're collecting litter!

We're changing light bulbs to save electricity.

7 Chimps

6 Bears

We bundle
our newspapers
for recycling.
THE BEAR NEWS

We're learning about recycling.
2

5 Leopards

4 Rhinos

We use
rechargeable
batteries.

We plant trees.

3 Pandas

2 Whales

We're watching for polluters.

I'm enjoying
the earth.

1 Elephant

Do You Want to Know More?

When people carpool or take the bus or train together, it cuts down on the number of vehicles polluting the air. Car exhaust harms the air and water. Biking and walking are good, pollution-free ways to travel.

Turning off the faucet while doing the dishes can save more than thirty gallons of water. Letting the water run while brushing your teeth can waste more than five gallons of water. Leaky faucets also contribute to water loss.

Recycled glass can be made into new bottles for beverages and jars for food. The glass is first sorted according to color: green, brown, and clear. Then it is broken into tiny pieces, melted, and mixed with new glass. More than 20 billion glass bottles and jars are discarded each year.

Cans that are not recycled will not become part of the earth again for 200 years. More than 65 billion soda cans are used each year. If the cans are recycled, they can be crushed, melted down, and made into solid bars of aluminum. The bars are pressed into aluminum sheets that are bought by can makers. Aluminum may be recycled again and again. Some communities also recycle aluminum foil, pie plates, frozen-food trays, and pet-food cans.

Litter contaminates the earth. Toxic things, such as paint and motor oil, soak into the land and harm the soil and water. Drinking water, fruits, and vegetables are damaged. Litter is also dangerous to wildlife. Animals and birds may be injured or die if they mistake litter, such as gum wrappers, for food.

Fluorescent light bulbs use 75 percent less electricity than incandescent bulbs. Energy-saving light bulbs are also helpful, because they use less electricity. When coal is burned to create electricity, harmful gases are released into the air. Using less electricity helps keep the air cleaner. Fluorescent light bulbs also last ten times longer than ordinary bulbs do. If fewer bulbs are used, there will be less garbage.

If all Sunday newspapers were bundled and recycled, over half a million trees would be saved each week. Cereal boxes, paper bags, magazines, and telephone books can also be recycled. Recycled paper is shredded and mixed with water to make pulp that is pressed into new sheets of paper and then dried.

You can learn to identify plastic recycling codes. These numbers—from 1 to 7—identify different types of plastics. Plastics numbered 1 and 2 are most commonly recycled. You can find these code numbers on the bottoms of containers marked for recycling. Soda, detergent, and shampoo bottles, water and milk jugs, and other plastic containers can be sorted according to their numbers. Many things, such as garbage cans and bags, pipes, hoses, fiberfill for sleeping bags and parkas, toys, car parts, and tennis-ball fuzz, can be made from recycled plastics.

Most batteries contain mercury, which is dangerous to the earth when thrown away. Rechargeable batteries contain cadmium, which is also harmful, but because rechargeable batteries can be used over and over again, fewer of them are discarded, creating less toxic waste.

Trees help keep the air clean by making oxygen and absorbing pollutants. More than one and a half billion trees are used each year for wood products, such as furniture and lumber for houses, and for paper products, including newspapers, books, and money.

Polluters are dangerous to oceans, beaches, and marine life. Garbage in the sand, such as pieces of glass or soda tabs, can injure people at the beach. Sea animals often mistake Styrofoam, plastic bags, and other wrappings for food. They die from eating this garbage. The plastic that holds six-packs together is especially dangerous because animals can get trapped in the rings. Clipping the rings apart can help prevent this.